The Heroic Women of Arnot

It was still dark outside, but a crowd of women was gathering at the bottom of the hill that led to the mines. Rosie counted the women. Twenty. Thirty. Forty. Fifty. Six—

"Rosie!"

Rosie turned around and hugged her cousin. "Mary! Isn't it great? There must be at least a hundred women here. It really is like an army, isn't it?"

"Aren't you two the Wilson daughters?" The warmth in Mother Jones's voice surprised them.

"We sure are," Rosie said proudly.

"Glad to have you marching with us." She patted Mary on the shoulder, then pulled a red cloth from her dress pocket and handed it to Rosie. "Tie this to your broom. Then the scabs will see you coming."

Mother Jones turned to the crowd. "Let's get moving!"

Rosie's mother beat on her dishpan. "Fall in!" she cried. Rosie waved her banner. Mary lifted her cymbal. The women ran down the hill toward the mine, banging wooden spoons and rolling pins on garbage pails, hammering on dishpans and shouting, "Victory!"

TROUBLE AT THE MINES

Doreen Rappaport

illustrated by Joan Sandin

A BANTAM SKYLARK BOOK®
NEW YORK · TORONTO · LONDON · SYDNEY · AUCKLAND

RL3,007-011

*This edition contains the complete text
of the original hardcover edition.*
NOT ONE WORD HAS BEEN OMITTED.

TROUBLE AT THE MINES

*A Bantam Skylark Book / published by arrangement with
Harper & Row Publishers, Inc.*

PRINTING HISTORY
Harper & Row edition published April 1987

*Skylark Books is a registered trademark of Bantam Books, a division of
Bantam Doubleday Dell Publishing Group, Inc. Registered in U.S.
Patent and Trademark Office and elsewhere.*

Bantam edition / November 1989

ISBN 0-553-15764-7

Published simultaneously in the United States and Canada

---

*Bantam Books are published by Bantam Books, a division of Bantam
Doubleday Dell Publishing Group, Inc. Its trademark, consisting of
the words "Bantam Books" and the portrayal of a rooster, is Registered
in U.S. Patent and Trademark Office and in other countries. Marca
Registrada. Bantam Books, 666 Fifth Avenue, New York, New York
10103.*

PRINTED IN THE UNITED STATES OF AMERICA

OPM   0 9 8 7 6 5 4 3 2 1

For my mother

Contents

Acknowledgments

Lois McLean, who is preparing a biography of Mother Jones and generously shared her knowledge and insight; Louanne Kennedy, who let me into the life of a coal miner's daughter; Keith Dix, Institute for Labor Studies, West Virginia University; the staff of The Library at Simon's Rock of Bard College.

December 1898

The steam whistle screeched. Rosie Wilson stopped playing with her cousin Mary and ran down the alley toward her house screaming, "Ma, Ma!"

Mrs. Wilson was already out the door and running up the hill. So was Aunt Sally. Rosie and Mary ran after them. Every man, woman and child in the town of Arnot, Pennsylvania, feared the sound of the steam whistle. The whistle meant an accident in the coal mines. It often meant death. Rosie's father, her two

1

brothers and her Uncle Jack worked in the mines, deep down in the earth where the coal lay buried.

"What happened?" Rosie's mother asked the mine superintendent when she and Aunt Sally reached the top of the hill.

"A part of a tunnel roof in the north section caved in," he said.

"Who's trapped?" Mrs. Wilson asked fearfully.

"We don't know yet."

Please don't let Pa be trapped, Rosie pleaded to God. Or Willie or Henry. She closed her eyes to block out the images of coal and rock crashing down on them.

The noon sun hid behind a cloud, robbing the winter day of its little warmth, but the women and children of Arnot did not go home. Rosie pulled her thin shawl over her long brown hair and stood next to her mother. Her cousin Mary and her three brothers huddled next to their mother. No one talked.

For the next three hours, they watched as men and boys came up out of the mines, their faces and clothing black as the coal below. Finally Rosie's brothers, Henry and Willie, came up. Rosie and her mother ran to them. Tired and damp from hours of trying to dig out their fellow miners, they hardly responded to their embraces. "Is your father safe?" Mrs. Wilson whispered.

"I don't know," Henry answered.

At four o'clock three men carried out the body of Barnell Cox. Mrs. Cox's shriek pierced the silence. Mrs. Wilson pulled Rosie tightly to her.

Rosie's father and Uncle Jack were among the last men to come up. "Thank God," whispered Rosie's mother.

Stooped over and covered with coal dust, the brothers walked slowly to Superintendent Lincoln. "We can't work down there anymore!" Rosie's uncle yelled. "It's too dangerous. The walls cave in. The roofs collapse. You promised to brace them. You've got to do it before there's another accident."

Superintendent Lincoln chewed on a piece of tobacco. "Mine inspector was here last week, and he didn't notice anything."

Rosie's father clenched his teeth. "In the twenty-five years the mine's been operating, the inspectors haven't remedied one complaint."

"If you don't like it, Bryan"—the superintendent paused to spit out his tobacco—"get another job."

"No use talking to him," said Rosie's uncle. "Let's go home, Bryan." The two men started down the hill. Their wives and children followed in silence.

"It's time to talk to the men, Jack," Rosie's father said. "Make them understand that we've got to unionize. We've got to speak in one voice to the mine owners. It's the only way things'll ever change."

"It's not gonna be easy, Bryan," said Uncle Jack.

"We've got to try something, Jack. It's been seven years since we've had a raise."

"It's not going to be easy on the wives and children," Uncle Jack said.

"It's not easy on us now," said Aunt Sally, "what with worrying that we'll lose you in the mines and barely having enough to pay our bills."

"Our sons in those black pits from the time they're seven," added Rosie's mother. "What kind of life is this for boys twelve and fourteen?"

"And before you know it, our three boys'll be going down into the mines, too," said Aunt Sally.

"I don't know a miner's wife who feels different," Rosie's mother said.

"What do you say, Jack, let's meet after supper and talk about it?"

"I guess it's as good a time as any," said Uncle Jack. The brothers shook hands, and the two families parted.

The house was cold. Rosie's mother filled up the stove with coal, and when it warmed up some, she heated the carrots and potatoes. Rosie set the table and sliced the bread. Her older brother Henry brought in water from the well, and the men began to try to wash off the coal dust stuck in the pores of their faces and hands.

Mrs. Wilson put the food on the table. "For

all that you give us tonight, Lord, we are grateful," she said.

"I'm glad we're all feeling so grateful,"
Rosie's father said. "Better remember it, 'cause
there may be hard times ahead."

"What do you mean, Pa?" asked Rosie.

"Well, last year when those miners near Pittsburgh banded together to stop that pay cut—"

"Cutting a miner's pay?" Henry interrupted.
"That's impossible. Taking nothing away from
nothing is nothing." Everyone laughed.

"True enough," Mr. Wilson said, "but when
those miners demanded their pay not be cut,
the first thing the company did was fire the
ringleaders to scare the others. And when that
didn't work, they evicted people from their
homes. Now this shack, flimsy and broken-
down as it is, is the only home we've got. But
it's owned by the company, and if the mine
owners want us out, they can evict us."

"But where would we go?" Rosie asked.

"Might have to sleep outside. Like those miners' families did. Slept outside in tents. It was hard going." He reached for some bread. "Might have been catastrophic if Mother Jones hadn't come to town. That feisty old lady got the brilliant idea of marching the strikers' children through Pittsburgh. It sure shocked people to see children in bitter-cold weather dressed in thin clothes and rags. Shocked them even more when they learned they were sleeping outdoors. Once it got in the newspapers, everyone was up in arms. The mine owners didn't know what hit 'em. Made them squirm to have folks learn how evil they were."

"If Mother Jones comes here, I'll march with her," Rosie said.

"I'm hoping it won't come to that," her father said. "I'm hoping it'll go easier here."

Rosie and Mary stared at the small plot of land squeezed between the houses. "There's no way this garden can grow enough food for us to live on," said Rosie.

"It better," said her mother, "because with your pa fired, it's only a matter of time before your brothers are fired. We're gonna need this food."

"If they keep firing people, there won't be anybody left to work the mines," said Mary.

"The mine owners don't intend to fire everybody and cripple production," Rosie's mother

9

said. "They're retaliating against Pa and Uncle Jack and the men who formed the union. Hoping that by firing the leaders, they'll scare others."

"Pa says lots of men are scared," Rosie said. "Over two hundred have packed up and left town."

"Right foolish of them," said Rosie's mother. "Won't be any different anywhere else. Same low wages and bad conditions in all the mines. They should stay here and fight."

"I'll fight, Ma," said Rosie.

"Me, too," said Mary.

"You can start right now by talking less and working more."

"Louann," Aunt Sally called, walking hurriedly up the alley.

"What is it, Sally?" Rosie's mother asked anxiously. "Have they fired Harry and Willie?"

"No firings today," Aunt Sally said. "But they've started evicting people, about thirty families so far. Bryan and Jack are going around getting people to take families in. They want us to fetch Sarah Cox and her children."

"Sarah Cox? The mine owners evicted her?" asked Mary.

"Sure did. Superintendent Lincoln came around this morning and told her she had no right to that house since her husband was dead and didn't work for the company anymore."

"How could they be that mean?" Rosie cried.

"They were even meaner to Bill Kennard's seventy-year-old mother. Lincoln told her she had to leave by tomorrow, even though Doc Walters said it might kill her."

"Guess the mine owners thought the firings didn't scare us enough, and figured this would," Rosie's mother said.

"Well, they figured wrong," said Aunt Sally. "Everyone's real riled up now. More determined than ever to stick with the union."

"Then maybe some good will come of this," said Rosie's mother. "Girls, finish covering those seeds with earth. Then let's see what we can do for Mrs. Cox."

Rosie and Mary followed their mothers down the alley. Outside the Coxes' shack stood a few rickety chairs and boxes. The two younger Cox boys were struggling to lug the kitchen table out the door. "Go help them," Aunt Sally told Mary and Rosie.

Rosie's mother stepped into the house. Mrs. Cox was taking down a picture of the Madonna and Child from the wall. "Can you imagine, Louann?" she said. "Barnell worked in those mines for twenty years, since he was twelve, and these few sticks of furniture are all the children and I have to show for it."

Rosie's mother put her arm on Mrs. Cox's shoulder, and they stood in silence. Finally Mrs. Wilson said, "Sarah, you can stay with us until you find a new place to live."

"That's kind of you, Louann, but you don't have enough room for your own family."

"We have enough, Sarah."

"The girls can sleep with me on the floor," Rosie added.

"Rosie's right," her mother said. "There's plenty of room for you and the girls."

"And your two boys will stay with us," Aunt Sally said.

"That settles it, Sarah," Rosie's mother said. "You're coming with us."

Rosie and Mary helped Rosie's mother carry a mattress. Aunt Sally picked up the pots and pans. Mrs. Cox took a long last look around the room, sighed deeply and turned to leave. Standing in the doorway was Miriam Kelsey, a miner's wife. She held out a sack of potatoes. "Sarah, take this."

"I can't, Miriam," Mrs. Cox said. "You hardly have enough for your own, now that John's been fired."

"Take it Sarah." Mrs. Kelsey's voice was firm. "John and I want you to have it." She placed the bag in Mrs. Cox's arms.

"Thank you, Miriam." Mrs. Cox's voice cracked. She embraced her neighbor. "Thank you."

Rosie stared at the bag of potatoes. She knew that the Kelseys would eat very little for dinner tonight. And with Mrs. Cox and her daughters living with her, Rosie knew she would be eating that much less too.

Mary put down her sewing. "Every time I think I've reached the end of this skirt, I find out I've only reached another seam."

"We'll be sewing till doomsday if our Pas and my brothers aren't rehired soon," said Rosie.

"Ma says Superintendent Lincoln wouldn't be meeting with the union today if the mine owners weren't ready to give in."

"I hope so," Rosie said. "I'm tired of eating cold potatoes."

"Sewing is worse than cold potatoes," said Mary.

"The only good thing about the past two months has been that with so many families leaving town, the boys are forced to ask us to play baseball," said Rosie.

Mary laughed. "Baseball beats sewing and cold potatoes."

"Are you girls finished with the basting?" Aunt Sally asked from across the room.

"Not yet, Ma," answered Mary.

"The meeting sure is lasting a long time," Aunt Sally said. "That's a good sign."

"I hope it's settled today," Rosie's mother said, "because with Henry and Willie fired too, this pile of sewing isn't enough to feed us and there's not much in the garden yet." She sighed. "Must say, I was relieved last week when Sarah Cox's sister sent for her and the children. We just didn't have enough to go around most nights."

Just then, Rosie's father and uncle walked into the house.

"How did it go?" Rosie's mother asked nervously.

"Did you get the raise?" asked Rosie.

Rosie's father slumped onto a crate. Uncle Jack stood in the middle of the room shaking his head.

"Girls, make your Pas some tea," Rosie's mother said. "What happened, Bryan?"

"Nothing good," he muttered. "First Lincoln kept us waiting for two hours. And when he finally let us into his office, he was all smiles. 'What can I do for you, boys?' he asked, as if he didn't know. We told him first he had to rehire everyone he fired, and then give us all a raise. Told him we got kids to feed, rent to pay, bills to meet, and we can't do it earning the same money as seven years ago."

"And what did he say?" asked Aunt Sally.

"He said, 'The company's not making enough money to give you boys a raise.' When he said that, Jack showed him the front page of the *Pittsburgh Daily*. Showed him that the newspaper said that the price of coal had doubled since last year. Told him, 'The company's making twice as much money, and we want more too.' Lincoln laughed. Leaned back in his chair and laughed. Then he dismissed us. Said there was nothing else to talk about and that he wouldn't be meeting with us again."

"What are you going to do now?" Aunt Sally asked.

"We're asking the men to go on strike," Rosie's father said.

"Isn't there any other way?" asked Aunt Sally.

"I can't see one," Rosie's father said. "They fired over two hundred men. They evicted fifty families. They refused to meet with the union for three months, and when they finally did meet with us today, it was only to tell us that they're not negotiating. If they won't negotiate, what choice do we have but to strike?"

"I'm scared, Pa," Rosie said.

Her father took her hand. "We're all scared, Rosie. But sometimes even when you're scared, you've got to act. We've got to act now and stand up for our rights."

"But what if the strike doesn't work?" asked

Rosie's mother. "What if you strike and they still don't give you a raise?"

"It'll work," Uncle Jack said. "It worked over in Cambria County. After months of not getting anywhere, the miners went on strike and they got their raise."

"How long do you think the strike'll last?" asked Aunt Sally.

"Not very long," Rosie's father said. "It's June now. Lots of coal has to be dug in the next few months to be ready for winter. The mine owners need us."

"I hope you're right, Bryan," said Rosie's mother.

Hundreds of people were sitting in the open field outside the town waiting for the union meeting to begin. Most of them were shouting at each other.

Uncle Jack was yelling at Rosie's father. "It's four months since this strike began. Over four hundred miners have left town, and every day more are leaving. Soon there won't be any union members left. We've got to go back to work, Bryan."

"We'll never get a raise if we go back."

"Brother, if this strike continues, there's not going to be anybody left in town to use the raise."

Rosie's father grabbed his brother's forearm. "Jack, we're close to winning. All the miners in towns around are out on strike. Production is crippled. If the mine owners don't give in soon, they won't be able to get the coal for winter. We just *have* to hold out a little longer."

"Lincoln told me they've got enough coal stocked from last spring to sell through this winter. They don't need us," shouted Uncle Jack. "He also told me that if this strike continues, the mine owners are going to close the mines permanently. Then we won't need a union."

"Lincoln tells you a story, and you believe him. You're a fool, Jack." Rosie's father raised his clenched fist so near Uncle Jack's face that Rosie and Mary were sure he was going to punch him.

"You're the fool, Bryan," said Uncle Jack. He turned and marched to the front of the gathering. "Friends, friends!" he shouted. "It's been four months since the strike began. Four months ago we had a little money, and there were plenty of vegetables in the garden. Now it's almost November and we have only cabbages and sprouts left. We have no money. We can't buy food for our families. We can't pay our rent. Winter's almost here. We can't get coal to heat our houses. We have no choice but to go back to work before our families starve and freeze to death!"

Uncle Jack held up a piece of paper. "See this paper? One hundred miners, two ministers, the town doctor, the druggist, the teacher . . . signed this petition asking the owners to open the mines so we can go back to work. They've agreed. Tomorrow morning the mines will be open and anyone who wants to go back to work can. I say it's time to go back to work, before we all starve."

Rosie's mother sprang to her feet. "Don't listen to Jack," she pleaded. "If you go back now, the mine owners will never give you a raise."

Aunt Sally stood up. "I think Jack is wrong. Things will only get better if we stick together. We can't buckle under to the mine owners."

Uncle Jack hollered. "Shut up, woman. If we don't go back tomorrow, the company will shut the mines down permanently, and we won't have any jobs to go back to."

"Mine owners always threaten to close the mines down when miners ask for what they deserve!" Aunt Sally yelled back.

"What do *you* know?" Uncle Jack shouted. "You're a woman, not a miner."

Rosie's mother pointed her finger at Uncle Jack. "Scab!"

"Fool!" Uncle Jack yelled.

"Scab!"

"Fool!"

Everyone began shouting at each other. The yelling accelerated to a roar. Only Rosie's father was quiet. He scanned the crowd frantically. "Who are you looking for, Pa?" asked Rosie, pulling on his arm.

"She's come," he whispered suddenly, pointing to an old woman walking slowly across the field toward Uncle Jack.

The woman was short, with thick round glasses, a round face and a round body. Her white hair was covered by a wide-brimmed hat. She wore a long-sleeved black dress with a frilly collar.

By the time she reached Uncle Jack, the shouting had stopped. "What do you think,

Mother Jones?" Rosie's father called out to her. "What should we do?"

Mother Jones clasped her hands and looked up as if in prayer. Then she looked out at the crowd, and her face broke into a slow grin. "Well," she said, "the first thing I think we should do is straighten Jack out. He's forgotten how important women are. He wouldn't be here today if it hadn't been for his mother."

Rosie and Mary looked at each other and giggled.

Amens and shrieks of laughter sounded all around them.

Her smile disappeared. "Jack has also forgotten how a miner's wife bids good-bye to her husband and sons every morning, never knowing if they'll be carried home mangled or dead. How she has to live in an overcrowded shack that's always dirty from coal dust. How she has to juggle her husband's meager wages to feed and clothe her family. And if her husband is injured, how she has to go back to work four-teen hours a day in the mills, and still cook, clean and raise the family. How can anyone believe that this strike isn't as much a woman's business as a man's?"

"Tell it to him again!" cried Aunt Sally.

"Don't she speak the truth. . . ."

"Glory be, glory be . . ."

Women called out from all directions.

"I know how hard it is for you women," Mother Jones continued, "for I too have suffered. And I know how hard it is for you men. Mining at its best is wretched work—breathing coal dust and damp air, never seeing sunlight. Never knowing when the roof might collapse, crushing your back and legs or burying you alive. Standing in sulphur water that eats through your shoes and brings sores to your flesh. Swinging your pick and ax where the roofs are so low you have to stoop over until your back aches too much to ever straighten up. A lifetime of working fourteen hours a day and nothing to show for it."

All around Rosie and Mary women were sighing and nodding their heads in agreement. Some women were crying.

Mother Jones raised her arms. "I can't argue with Jack about how bad things are. This strike has been going on for four months, and the company hasn't budged. Some of you have been thrown out of your houses. There's little or no money to buy food. No one thought it would last this long. I understand why you think going back to work is the only choice."

"Why shouldn't we?" a voice cried out.

"Because if you do," Mother Jones replied, "things will never change! Let's look at the facts. You're on strike because you're earning the same money today as you earned seven years ago. Seven years is a long time to go without a pay raise."

Her pointed finger swung in an arc around the field. "If you go back to work now, it will be for the same low wages and long hours." She lowered her voice to almost a whisper. Rosie and Mary leaned forward so as not to miss a word. "You'll die in the mines. Your sons will die in the mines and so will your grandsons. And you won't even have enough money to bury them.

"You've got to stick together. If your brothers

in other mines can stay out, *you* can stay out. If they can go hungry, *you* can go hungry. If their children can go hungry, *your* children can go hungry." Rosie squeezed Mary's hand.

Mother Jones stretched out her arms again, her voice soaring like the preacher's on Sunday. "You've got to rise and pledge to stick to your brothers until this strike is won."

Rosie's father and mother rose. Then Aunt Sally. Rosie's brother Henry stood up and began clapping and stamping his feet. Rosie and Mary jumped up and down, striking their hands together as fast and as hard as they could. One by one, other men, their wives and children by their sides, stood up. The clapping swelled until it was deafening.

Mother Jones wasn't finished yet. "At five o'clock tomorrow morning," she yelled, "I want every woman to meet me at the bottom of the hill. You men stay home and take care of the children for a change. We'll take care of any man who dares to go back to work. I want every woman to come and bring a mop, a broom, or a dishpan. Our army will make sure that no one goes into the mines." She dropped her arms and began to sing.

"Bring the good old bugle, boys!
We'll sing another song;
Sing it with a spirit
That will start the world along...."

The crowd joined in, and the meeting ended in a burst of song.

Rosie's mother hugged her. "That's why mine owners call Mother Jones the most dangerous woman in America," she said.

She sure can talk, Rosie thought, but the part about the brooms and mops and the army, that was crazy.

"I must compliment you ladies." Mother Jones walked up to them. "You sure did teach those men something about courage." She took Aunt Sally's hand. "Not easy standing up like that in front of everyone, defying your husband."

"Sure wasn't," Aunt Sally said softly.

"I was stopped by the sheriff before coming to this meeting," Mother Jones continued. "He told me he had a warrant, and if I went anywhere near those mines, he'd have me arrested. Now I don't mind being arrested." She grinned. "Some of the most patriotic Americans I know have fought for justice and ended up in jail. But I don't think it would be good strategy right now to end up in jail. So one of you ladies will have to lead the army tomorrow."

"Louann had better do it," Aunt Sally said. "Jack didn't stand with the rest of us. I may have my hands full tomorrow morning with him."

"I'll gladly do it," said Rosie's mother.

"Then it's settled," Mother Jones said. "Now get your daughters home so they can get some sleep and march with us tomorrow."

October 16, 1899

It was still dark outside, but Rosie's mother was rushing around the house, banging a hammer on an old tin dishpan. "Hurry up, darlin'! Hurry up, and don't forget the broom." Rosie jumped out of bed. She dressed hurriedly, grabbed her broom and raced after her mother.

A crowd of women was gathering at the bottom of the hill that led to the mines. Rosie looked around for Mary but couldn't find her.

She noticed a few of the older girls from school standing with their mothers.

Mother Jones's voice boomed as she made her way through the crowd. "How you doing? Right glad to see you. You sure look dangerous."

Rosie counted the women. Twenty. Thirty. Forty. Fifty. Six—

"Rosie!"

Rosie turned around and hugged her cousin. "Mary! Where have you been? I've been looking for you. Isn't it great? There must be at least a hundred women here. It really is like an army, isn't it?"

Mary pulled her cousin away from the crowd. "Pa left the house before anybody was up," she whispered. "He went back to work."

"I don't believe you," Rosie yelled.

"Shh! Ma told us she won't let him in the house as long as he's a scab. I never saw her so mad. Rosie, I'm scared."

"Now why are you two huddling over here?" The warmth in Mother Jones's voice surprised them. "Aren't you two girls the Wilson daughters?"

"We sure are," Rosie said proudly. Mary looked down at the ground.

"Glad to have you marching with us." She patted Mary on the shoulder. "Right good cymbal," she said, looking at Mary's dishpan. "The scabs'll sure hear you coming." She pulled out a red cloth from her dress pocket and handed it to Rosie. "Tie this to your broom. Then the scabs will see you coming."

"Mother Jones," Rosie's mother said, "I think everyone who's coming is here."

"Then let's get moving." Mother Jones turned to the crowd. "Friends, I can't go with you to the mines," she said. "I've been threatened with arrest if I do. But you don't need me. Louann Wilson will lead the army. Don't be afraid of anyone. When you see those scabs, hammer and howl. Hammer and howl. Use your mops, use your brooms and chase those men away."

Rosie's mother beat on her dishpan. "Fall in!" she cried. The women lined up behind her.

"Let's go," Rosie said to Mary, lifting her banner as high as she could.

"We will never retreat!" chanted Rosie's mother.

"We will never retreat!" cried Rosie.

"We will never retreat!" shouted Mary.

"We will never retreat." The women picked

up the refrain and followed Rosie's mother
along the creek and up the steep hill that led to
the mines.

> "We will never retreat,
> There's sixty blisters on my feet.
> My nose is burned a handsome red.
> I'm covered o'er with dust.
> We'll win this strike or bust."

When they reached the top of the hill, they saw about fifteen men sorting coal and loading it onto the railroad cars. Rosie saw Uncle Jack harnessing a mule. "Mary," she whispered, "there's your pa."

Mary didn't respond. Rosie saw tears in her cousin's eyes.

"Let's get them!" Rosie's mother shouted, banging hard on her dishpan.

"Let's get them!" echoed the women.

But before they could go any farther, they were stopped by the sheriff and two deputies.

Rosie's mother smiled. "Sheriff, what are you doing here?"

"I might ask the same of you ladies," he answered.

"We're here to keep those scabs from working and to close down the mines."

"I can't let you do that, ma'am. You didn't hire these men, so you can't fire them. You don't own the mines, so you can't close them."

"The lives and sweat of our men own those mines, Sheriff," said Rosie's mother.

"According to the law, ma'am, you're trespassing on private property. If you don't leave, I'll have to—"

"Shoot us?" Rosie blurted out.

"Rosie," her mother said. "How could you say that? The sheriff wouldn't do anything awful like that, would you, Sheriff?" She banged her hammer on her dishpan, and it resounded like a cymbal. "Fall in," she ordered.

"My dear lady, you're making too much noise," the sheriff said. "Remember the mules. You're going to frighten them."

"Sheriff, *you* remember the mules." Rosie's mother lunged forward, whirling her tin dishpan over her head. The sheriff lost his balance and fell into the creek. Rosie and Mary laughed. Aunt Sally laughed. The whole army laughed as it advanced toward the two deputies. The sheriff's men took off down the hill.

"Fall in!" Rosie's mother cried. Rosie waved her banner. Mary lifted her cymbal. The women ran down the hill toward the scabs, banging wooden spoons and rolling pins on garbage pails, hammering on dishpans and shouting, "Victory!"

When the scabs saw the women rushing toward them, they mounted the mules to flee. But the mules bucked and kicked, threw their drivers off and galloped down the hill with the scabs running after them. The women followed, flailing their weapons and shouting, "Victory, victory!"

When Aunt Sally caught up with Uncle Jack, she grabbed him from behind. He fell down hard and lay so still that Rosie thought he was dead. Aunt Sally leaned over him and shook his shoulders. "Jack, get up!" Uncle Jack blinked his eyes. Aunt Sally shook him again. "Jack Wilson, swear to me you'll never scab again."

Uncle Jack opened his eyes and saw women all around him. "Well, Jack?" Aunt Sally demanded.

He swallowed hard. "I swear," he said.

Aunt Sally sighed with relief. "I'm glad you've come to your senses, Jack." She offered her hand to help him up.

"I'm glad too, Pa," Mary whispered.

"Are there any men working underground?" asked Rosie's mother.

"No. We were just getting ready to go down with the mules when you arrived."

"We'd better stay here in case any of those scabs try to sneak back into the mines," Rosie's mother said.

"Can't speak for all the scabs," Aunt Sally said, "but I sure know Jack Wilson won't show his face here again."

The women laughed and positioned themselves at the mine entrance, their mops and brooms and pails and rolling pins poised at their sides, ready for battle. Rosie wedged her broom into the earth, retied her red banner at the top, and waited for further orders. Mary stood next to her, holding her cymbal ready.

> *"We will never retreat,*
> *We will never retreat. . . ."*

Rosie loved the women's voices. "I bet they can hear us in town," she told Mary proudly.

"Did you see those mules balk when the men tried to mount them?" Mary asked.

"Mules know better than to scab, even if men don't," Rosie said.

"I never saw my pa run so fast in my whole life," said Mary. The two girls shrieked with laughter at the image of Uncle Jack and the other men tearing down the hill.

"What's going on with you two?" asked Aunt Sally.

"Well . . ." Mary tried to answer, but she couldn't stop laughing.

As the morning passed, the army of women kept getting bigger and bigger. And with each new arrival the women retold the story of the morning's events. Mother Jones sent word that she had told the men to arrange a parade that night.

As the afternoon sky clouded over, the women lit fires to warm themselves and shared what little food they had. At twilight a woman came to tell them that the parade was about to begin.

"Shouldn't someone stay and guard the mines?" Rosie asked.

"I don't think anyone will be coming back tonight," her mother answered. "Let's go, everyone!"

The army of women began walking down the hill toward the town. "Look." Mary pointed to the parade in the distance. "It's like a long snake with red, white and blue fangs."

"Where did they get all those flags?" Rosie cried excitedly.

"Must be thousands," said Mary.

"It's better than the Fourth of July," Rosie exclaimed.

In the center of town people were embracing each other, shouting, "Hello, brother, hello, sister, bless the union," and waving signs reading NO WORK TOMORROW and UNITED WE STAND.

"There's Pa," Rosie cried, inching her way through the crowd toward her father.

"And Uncle Jack." Rosie's mother embraced Aunt Sally. "It's good to have him with us again, Sally."

A trumpet rallied the crowd to attention. Mother Jones, her face triumphant, stood on the steps of the Opera House. "Friends," she

began, "it's been a glorious day." As the crowd
cheered, Mother Jones began to sing.

> *"Praise God, from whom all blessings flow,*
> *Praise him, all creatures here below;*
> *Praise him above, ye heavenly host . . ."*

Everyone joined in, their voices surging.
"I don't know if the Lord intended it, but

'Old Hundredth' is as good a victory song as any," Mother Jones shouted, and the crowd applauded wildly.

"It is I who must applaud you," Mother Jones continued. "For today, by your courageous acts, we triumphed. But I caution you. The battle is not yet won. The strike is not yet over. But with our army behind us, we cannot lose.

"Praise God, from whom all blessings flow,"

she sang loudly, and the crowd sang with her.

"Now that we've thanked the Lord properly, let's sing and dance so loudly that we wake up the mine owners wherever they're hiding and remind them who they're up against. All three of Arnot's bands are with us tonight, and they have practiced a very special tune for you, so let's hear from them."

The fiddles and trumpets let go with a lively

two-step. The cousins joined hands and whirled around and around.

"You girls want to see the parade from up here?" Uncle Jack shouted, gesturing to his shoulders. Rosie and Mary nodded, and their fathers hoisted them up on their shoulders.

Up on top, among a sea of red, white and blue, Rosie lifted her broom and shouted, "Ready to wake up the mine owners?"

Mary whacked her dishpan. "I'm ready!"

Down the street their fathers carried them, and they sang along with everyone as loud as they could:

"My Country, 'tis of thee,
Sweet land of liberty,
Of thee I sing.
Land where my fathers died,
Land of the Pilgrims' pride,
From e-ev-'ry-y mountainside
Le-et freedom ring."

October 17, 1899

Rosie woke up and looked around the empty room. She dressed quickly and went into the kitchen. Her father was drinking a cup of black coffee.

"Where is everybody?" Rosie asked, pouring herself some coffee.

"Your ma's up at the mines with the women. Henry's out with Uncle Jack."

Rosie reached into a bowl for some bread scraps. "Why didn't Ma wake me to go with her?"

"We thought you needed the sleep. Yesterday was a long day. We didn't get home from the parade until early in the morning."

"Wasn't it great, Pa? Wasn't it great? All those people and banners and singing. I wish Willie had been here instead of in Clearfield. He would have loved it. Especially Mother Jones! I never heard anybody speak like her in my life."

"Sure is true, she does have the gift of the gab." He rubbed his right forefinger across his top lip. "I don't know what us miners would do without her."

There was a knock at the door, and Mother Jones walked into the kitchen. "Superintendent Lincoln gave notice to the Kanes and Bouncers early this morning that they have to find a new home by tomorrow," she said excitedly. "It looks like there's going to be another round of evictions."

Rosie's father sighed.

"Bryan, there's no time for sighing. You've got work to do. The company got a writ from some judge to chase the women away from the mines, so you'd better get out there and talk to the men who went to work yesterday. Make sure they're not going back tomorrow. I'm going to drive over to Blossburg and thereabouts to find people who'll shelter the evicted and feed the rest of us."

"Can I go with Mother Jones?" Rosie asked her father.

Mother Jones nodded to Mr. Wilson. "I don't see why not," he said.

"Can Mary come too, Mother Jones?" Rosie asked.

"If you find her real fast."

Rosie raced out the door. By the time she returned with Mary, the horse was hitched up to the wagon and ready to go. Mary and Rosie climbed up next to Mother Jones. Mother Jones lifted the reins.

"Where're we going, Mother Jones?" Mary asked.

"To every farmer within ten miles," she said. "We need their help."

They drove past the miners' shacks and over the hill to where the Pennsylvania country broke into rich farmland. The fields were bare now, but occasionally there was a golden stalk of corn sticking up as a reminder of the riches that had been reaped.

"Down this road is Tom Benson's farm," Rosie said. "Pa says he does pretty well."

"We'll drive up to the house," Mother Jones said. "Might catch him there, or even better, catch his wife. I always find the women understand much quicker what's right and what's wrong."

Mother Jones stopped the horse in front of a sprawling clapboard farmhouse with lots of windows and a front porch. Rosie had never seen anything so grand. The two girls jumped down from the wagon and walked toward the front of the house.

"Come around here, girls." Mother Jones led them to the back of the house. She knocked on a sturdy wooden door.

"Who's there?" The man's voice was gruff.

"It's Mary Harris Jones, sir."

"Who?"

"Mary Harris Jones, from over in Arnot. Like to come in and talk with you, if I may."

A tall gray-haired man with a ruddy face opened the door. "Yeah? Well, what do you want?"

"Would find it easier to talk to you if we were in the same room," said Mother Jones. The farmer looked Mother Jones up and down.

Rosie wasn't sure he'd let them into the house.

"All right," he said, "but I don't have much time."

Rosie, Mary and Mother Jones stepped into the kitchen. There was a warm fire in the stove, and smells of meat and vegetables filled Rosie's nostrils and set off her hunger.

A robust woman, stirring something in a pot at the stove, looked up and said, "Good morning."

"Good morning," Mother Jones said. "My name is Mary Harris Jones. My friends call me Mother Jones. I've come to talk with you about the miners' strike in Arnot."

"I know all about it," the farmer said. "The mine owners came by last month. Told us all about the strike."

"Did they now?" Mother Jones said. "Did they tell you that they have given a raise to miners in other counties, and for some reason none of us can figure out, they've refused to give our men the same? Did they tell you that they were evicting miners and their families from their homes? Did they tell you that most miners' families are living on scraps? Did they tell you that, sir?" Mother Jones's face turned red.

"Why don't you sit down, ma'am?" the farmer's wife said quickly.

"Don't worry about me, ma'am. Worry about the women and their children. Like Mary and Rosie here. Their fathers have been out of work six months. Their mothers took in sewing, but that ran dry. Rosie's brother Henry got lucky and found a job this summer for a farmer. Her brother Willie left home to work in the Clear-field mines. Sends home every penny he earns; and it ain't much more than pennies, but it helps some to feed them. They're luckier than Mary's family, where nobody's working." Mother Jones paused. "I think it's important that we give to our neighbors in times of need, don't you?"

The woman looked toward her husband, anxious for him to speak, but he didn't. "Would you folks like some food?" she asked. "I've got a nice corn soup on the stove." Rosie could taste it in her mouth.

"No, ma'am," Mother Jones said. "I thank you for your generosity, but we're not here to get food for ourselves. We're here to get food for our neighbors."

"I think we could—" the woman said.

But her husband interrupted her. "Don't see that this strike is any business of ours."

Mother Jones walked to the window. "You got beautiful land out here, beautiful, rich soil. But I bet some years the spring rains are too hard, or the summer's too dry, or the fall frost too early, and then the harvest isn't too good. Maybe you don't even grow enough to sell, just enough to feed the cows and chickens. Maybe you even have to borrow some, and you worry about paying the high interest back. In those times it's good to know there are friends out there to help."

"Tom, if charity don't start at home, where does it start?"

"What is it you need?" The farmer's voice was still gruff.

"I was kind of hoping we might be able to come back on a regular basis and get some eggs," said Mother Jones. "Not so many as would cripple you for the selling, just some of the surplus. And how about some corn?"

"Only corn I got is feed corn for the cows," said the farmer.

"It would be a lot better than eating scraps," Mother Jones said. She looked around the kitchen. "Mighty nice house you got here. Looks real big from the outside. You must have lots of kids to fill it up."

The woman hesitated. "No. Our three boys are all married now and live in their own places, down the road a piece."

"All this space and no children. Well then I wonder if it's possible that you might not offer some space to some of our mining families who've been evicted and have no place to go."

"Well, I don't know," the farmer said.

"Well, I do," the woman said. "We've got room here for one family. A man and his wife and two children."

"But they'll have to work," the man insisted.

"I'm sure they wouldn't have it any other way," Mother Jones said. "Well, this sure has been a pleasant visit. You sure are generous folk, and I can't tell you how grateful I am. Our friends will be coming by tomorrow morning. We have to go now. We have lots more ground to cover." Mother Jones reached her right hand out to the woman, who grabbed it. "Thank you, ma'am." She offered her hand to the farmer. "Thank you, sir." He took it hesitantly.

Rosie, Mary and Mother Jones climbed back into the wagon. "Well," Mother Jones said, "I knew he wasn't as tough as he looked." She paused. "I know you were both smelling that food and praying you could have some, but I couldn't let you take it when she offered it."

"But why?" Rosie asked, feeling the hunger all over again.

"I didn't want them to think we came for our stomachs. As hungry as you are, there was something more important at stake than just your empty stomachs. Now let's get this horse moving. We've got lots of territory to cover."

It was past midnight when Mother Jones turned the wagon into Arnot. Rosie struggled to keep her eyes open and remember the day. They had gone from farm to farm, and Mother Jones had convinced almost everyone they visited to give food to the miners. Many people had offered their homes to the evicted. Rosie had never realized how generous people could be.

December 1899

Rosie lingered over her soup. "You'd better eat up if you want to be on time for the parade," her mother told her.

Since Mother Jones had arrived two months ago, there had been a parade every evening. The night before, over one thousand people had marched. Rosie was tired of marching in the cold night, tired of waving her banner and tired of singing patriotic songs. She was even tired of Mother Jones's speeches.

"I don't see as there's anything to parade about," Rosie said.

"Nothing to parade about? What about celebrating the new shipment of food that Mother Jones got from the farmers near Pittsburgh? And what about celebrating the money she raised?"

"The food and money won't last forever, Ma. And with Willie fired from the Clearfield mines and you having hardly any sewing, we may starve."

"Now where did you get such a silly idea? We're not going to starve. When the money's gone, Mother Jones'll go out and raise some more. She sure knows how to get people to empty their pockets." Her mother chuckled. "And aside from what Mother Jones has done, what about celebrating what *we've* done? Today we convinced two more miners not to go back to work."

"Two more miners? Ma, for the last two

months we've been out there every morning and evening pleading and hollering and praying and singing, and there are still thirty-nine men working."

"Thirty-nine men can't do the work of one thousand," Rosie's mother snapped. "And it won't be thirty-nine for long. Right now your pa's out talking to Mr. Kennard and his three sons. With them coming over, that'll only be thirty-five. Now eat up."

Rosie made no gesture toward her soup. Mrs. Wilson laid down her sewing, walked over to her daughter and put her arms around her. "I know it's been hard, Rosie, what with the mine owners closing the school these two months, and you standing outside every morning and evening in the bitter cold and not having enough to eat. And with Mary being so sick the last three weeks..."

The door opened. Rosie's mother looked up. "How'd it go, Bryan?"

Rosie's father's voice was flat. "I convinced Bill Kennard and his sons not to go to work tomorrow."

"So why do you sound so glum?"

"Bill Kennard's not going back to work, but my brother Jack is."

"Uncle Jack?" Rosie asked.

"Sally'll throw him out again and he'll come to his senses," Mrs. Wilson said.

"'Fraid not. This time Sally agrees with him. She told me six months is just too long to be on strike, too long to live on bread and the occasional eggs and scraps of meat that Mother Jones rounds up."

"She doesn't mean it," Rosie's mother said. "She's just tuckered out from nursing Mary and the three little ones through smallpox. She hasn't slept more than a few hours the last three weeks. Scared out of her mind most of the time that they would die."

"She meant it, all right. You should have

heard her, screaming and hollering, 'I don't care what you say, Jack is going back to work 'cause I'm not letting my family starve to death!' "

"She's just feeling desperate. We've all been through it, but it passes. I'll go talk to her now."

"No, Louann, talking won't help. Sally's given up hope."

"Not Sally," Rosie's mother insisted.

"Even Sally," Rosie's father said. He shook his head. "When the men find out that Jack's been broken, more will follow."

"Let me get you something warm, dear. It'll soothe some. Rosie, finish up your soup. We can't be wasting the little we have."

"Rosie?"

"What, Pa?"

"With Uncle Jack and Aunt Sally going to the other side, you won't be seeing your cousins."

Mrs. Wilson placed a bowl of soup in front of her husband.

"Did you hear me?" Rosie's father asked.

"I heard you, Pa." Rosie's voice was barely audible.

"In strikes, we gotta take sides. Mary and her brothers will be taking their parents' side, and you and Henry and Willie will be taking ours. I don't want you playing or talking with your cousins anymore."

"But Pa—"

"No talking or playing anymore."

"Ma," Rosie pleaded.

"Pa's right, Rosie. I know not having your best friend with you is going to make you feel extra lonely, but we don't associate with traitors. Even if they are family."

Tears filled her mother's eyes.

"Mary's not a traitor," Rosie said.

"Finish your soup," her father said. He lifted his bowl to his mouth and drank the watery liquid.

"I'm not hungry." Rosie pushed her chair away from the table and started walking out of the room.

"Come back here and finish your soup!" her father shouted.

"Bryan, leave her be," Rosie's mother said. "She's just a little girl."

January 1900

It was quiet in Rosie's house. Her mother was out marching with the women. Her father and brothers were at a union meeting.

Someone knocked on the door. "Come in," Rosie called out. She turned around and saw Mother Jones. "No one's here," she said.

"Oh." Mother Jones dragged out the word as if she were thinking about something else. "Do you mind if I sit and rest a bit? It's bitter cold out there."

"Would you like a cup of coffee?" Rosie asked.

"That would be mighty fine," Mother Jones said, sitting down. "Haven't seen you out there much with the women lately."

"I—I haven't been feeling well," Rosie stammered.

"Nothing serious, I hope."

"Nothing too serious." Rosie avoided Mother Jones's eyes.

"Well, that's good. I was kind of thinking that maybe you haven't been marching because you're feeling discouraged. Hard not to get discouraged when the strike is in its seventh month."

Rosie poured the cold coffee into a cup without saying anything and handed it to Mother Jones.

Mother Jones sipped it slowly. "Everybody

starts out thinking the strike'll be over soon. And when it's not, and there's not much food on the table, and their children get sick and there's no money for medicine, well, they start feeling sorry for themselves. Thinking maybe the union isn't such a good idea. Thinking maybe it's better to go back to work than starve to death. Yup, they get to feeling real sorry for themselves and go back. I've known families where one brother's striking, the other brother's scabbing. The wives pass each other on the street and in church and never exchange a word."

"Yesterday I was out walking and saw my cousin Mary and her brothers." Rosie hesitated. "I wanted to say hello, but I'm not allowed."

Mother Jones nodded. "Yes, strikes can hurt the soul as much as the stomach." She rested the coffee cup on the table. "Thirty years ago, I was living in Memphis with my husband and four children. My husband was an iron molder and I was a teacher. We didn't have much, but we got along.

"Then a yellow-fever epidemic swept through Memphis. Rich people left town, but us poor folks didn't have any choice but to stay locked in our houses and pray we wouldn't take sick.

"I sat in my house listening to the cries of the dying in neighboring houses. Every morning there would be dead people lying in the street. Then, one by one, my four children got sick. I nursed them night and day, but they died anyway. Then my husband caught the fever and died too. I just sat in that house not caring whether I lived or died. Didn't go out for days. Then one morning I knew I couldn't sit there any longer. There were people who needed help. I got a nursing permit and went from house to house helping the sick.

"By the time the plague ended, I had figured out why so many people had died. They had died because they didn't have money. Didn't have money to buy a horse and wagon so they could leave town. Didn't have money for nurses and doctors. I got angrier and angrier thinking about it. Realizing that my family might have lived if we had had enough money. But knowing that couldn't bring them back."

"Will it ever be the way it was before the strike?" Rosie blurted out.

"Can't ever be," Mother Jones said. "We can't undo what's happened." She placed her hand on top of Rosie's hand. "It won't do you no good to sit in this house pitying yourself, Rosie. You've got to get out and march, and help your ma and pa hold on to their strength. You've got to think of someone other than yourself."

Mother Jones got up to leave. "I'll be looking for you out there, Rosie."

* * *

The women, rolling pins, brooms and dish-pans at their sides, were clustered at the bottom of the hill that led to the mines.

"Praise God, from whom all blessings flow . . ."

they sang. There were only thirty miners working now, but the women still came out every morning and evening, determined to convince them or shame them into not working.

Rosie watched Uncle Jack walking slowly down the hill, his right hand tightly clasping his lunch box.

"Why Jack Wilson, I'm ashamed to see you coming down that hill!" Rosie's mother yelled above the singing. "What are you doing up there, working for a pittance, when you could be down here starving with dignity?"

Uncle Jack kept on walking, his eyes downcast.

"Jack Wilson, I hear your own brother won't

talk to you anymore!" a woman shouted.

"Jack Wilson, don't you want the honor of joining the longest strike in the state of Pennsylvania? Or do you prefer the dishonor of being a scab?" another woman called out.

"Please don't go back to work tomorrow, Uncle Jack," Rosie pleaded. Uncle Jack didn't look up. Rosie's eyes followed the swing of his lunch box. Up and down. Up and down.

"Please don't go back to work tomorrow, Uncle Jack," she pleaded. The singing was more like shouting now.

"Praise him, all creatures here below . . ."

"Shut up!" Uncle Jack yelled. "All of you, shut up!"

"Blackleg!" someone yelled out.

"Blackleg!" Rosie taunted him.

Uncle Jack looked up and glared at his niece.

"Blackleg!" she screamed again.

He lunged toward Rosie and slapped her across the face.

Rosie flailed her arms frantically. "Blackleg!" He lunged at her again. "Blackleg, blackleg!" she screamed over and over again, her screams turning into heavy sobs.

Rosie's mother lowered her mop, charged at Uncle Jack's ribs and knocked him down. Two women pulled her back. Uncle Jack stumbled to his feet and ran. Mrs. Wilson ran to Rosie and put her arms around her, but she knew Rosie could not be comforted.

"Ma, my hands and feet are numb."

"Get the quilt from our bed and wrap it around your body," Rosie's mother said. "And wrap your hands loosely with a woolen scarf and rub them together. It'll break up the numbness some."

"What do I do for my feet?"

"Listen to that snow battering down the mountain and be thankful your feet aren't out there in the blizzard."

Suddenly the door opened. "The strike is over! The mine owners have given in," Willie shouted.

Mrs. Wilson dropped her sewing and stared at her son with disbelief.

"A half hour ago they called in Pa and the other men on the committee and told them we could have the raise."

Mrs. Wilson let out a deep breath. "Thank God, thank God," she sobbed. "We showed them, didn't we?"

"Yeah, Ma, we showed them," Willie said.

Rosie's eyes welled up with tears. "Oh, Ma, I'm so glad it's over."

"See," Mrs. Wilson said, stroking her daughter's face, "I told you that if we had faith, it would work out." She pulled both children to her. "Willie, where's your pa and Henry?"

"Henry and a few other men have gone to tell the miners living with families in Blossburg. Pa's with Mother Jones planning the biggest parade this town has ever seen."

"But it's a blizzard out there," Rosie said.

Her mother laughed. "Silly girl, to think a blizzard could stop us."

"Ma, I've got to be getting on and telling more folks," said Willie.

"Go on, then. We'll see you later at the parade."

Rosie ran into her room and pulled out the red cloth that Mother Jones had given her. Then she ran into the kitchen, picked up the broom and tied the cloth to it.

"We will never retreat!
We will never retreat! . . ."

Up went her broom as she skipped around the room. "Ma?" Rosie stopped skipping. "What will happen to Uncle Jack now that the strike's over?"

"Don't know, and don't care." Her mother's voice was sharp.

"But now that the strike's over, I can talk to Mary again, can't I?"

"I guess so," her mother muttered. "But I'm not sure your pa will allow her in the house. Now"—her voice was cheerful again—"put on more clothing. There's a blizzard outside, and we'll be out celebrating a long time."

"I don't feel cold anymore, Ma."

Her mother smiled. "When the soul's warm, the body's burning."

Out the door and down the alley they ran, knocking on doors and shouting, "Strike's over, strike's over!" Heads popped out of opened doors.

"Strike's over!"

"Hallelujah! Hallelujah!"

"Bless the union. . . ."

"Victory!"

Cheers resounded as men, women and children, flags in hands, filed out of their houses.

"Victory!" Rosie shouted, as she ran past Mary's darkened house. She wanted to knock on the door. She wanted to see Mary, but she didn't dare. She walked on.

The center of town was bulging with people and flags and noise.

Rrr-rrr-rrr, a drum rolled.

"Parade's about to begin!" a man shouted, offering Rosie a small flag. His face was gray, his body bent from years underground.

"I've got a banner. Thank you though." Rosie lifted it as high as she could.

"I'll take one, sir," said her mother.

Rrr-rrr-rrr, the drum sounded again.

The snow-filled sky erupted with color. From all directions iridescent blazes shot up. *Whoosh! Whoosh!* Rockets streaked reds and pinks and oranges across the white sky. *Whoosh! Whoosh!* Rosie followed pinwheels of blue and green light around and around until she was dizzy. A cannon roared. A rainbow stretched across the sky. A fan of gold, as brilliant as the sun, opened up. A field of red flowers exploded.

One of the miners, with the broadest smile Rosie had ever seen, rode by on a dapple-gray horse. Lengths of red, white and blue cloth hung down from the horse's neck. Attached to its brow band near its ears was an American flag.

"My country, 'tis of thee,"

the fiddlers played. *Whoosh! Whoosh!* Flares whizzed up.

"Sweet land of liberty,"

Rosie whooped along with the crowd.

"Of thee I sing."

The horse pranced around, its tail swinging back and forth in time.

"Land where my fathers died..."

The bugles opened up and drowned out the fiddles.

"Land of the Pilgrims' pride...

Hallelujah! Hallelujah!" The singing and shouting soared.

Rosie lifted her banner and joined the jubilant dancing and singing down the main street.

When the parade reached the opera house, the cannon roared again. Flags waved in tribute to Mother Jones and the union committee, who stood on the steps of the opera house.

"Bless the union, bless the union!" someone shouted, and the crowd picked up the chant. "Bless the union, bless the union..."

"Friends!" Rosie's father shouted over the noise. "Tonight we celebrate a great victory. A victory for every man and woman and child in Arnot who held out these past eight months.

"Praise God, from whom all blessings flow..."

he began, and the crowd sang with him.

"Yes, the Lord helped us in our struggle," Rosie's father went on, "but we couldn't have done it without our women. Brave women who encouraged us when we despaired, who spent every morning and evening singing and praying and shouting at those cowards who abandoned us, and then sewed and mended into the wee hours to put food on the table. We will not forget their strength, their courage, their love."

An urge to touch her mother overwhelmed Rosie, but she was too far from her.

"We must also pay tribute to a woman who aided us with tongue and brain and sympathy, and when necessary, with anger. They're still talking about it in Blossburg, how Mother Jones taught our neighbors the real meaning of charity. When we thought we'd starve, she got farmers to give us corn, eggs and beef. When we had no place to live, she got folks to open their homes to us. She raised more money for us than they've seen in the church coffers in many a year."

He led the crowd into a crescendo of cheering and clapping as Mother Jones stepped forward. "Well, my friends," she said, "it sure is a glorious night, despite the blizzard. A night that will go down in history. A night that your children and grandchildren will hear about. A night when the mine owners acknowledged the heroic courage of the men and women and children of Arnot.

"Soon you'll be back at work. There'll be food on your table. Coal in your stove to warm you. And a little more money in your pocket. But . . . you must never forget the hunger or the cold or the despair of these past eight months. You must never forget, for there'll be more struggles ahead. And remembering your pain and strength will help you when the next battle comes."

"Bless the union, bless the union . . ." Faster and faster, louder and louder, the cry pounded the air.

Mother Jones waited until it was quiet. "Some who started out with us aren't here tonight," she said.

"Cowards . . ."

"Traitors . . ."

Mother Jones's voice rose above the crowd as they vented their anger.

"Dear friends, they were frightened. Frightened by hunger, frightened by sickness, they betrayed their brothers and sisters." She paused. "But we fought for them anyway, and we have won for them too. And now that we're victorious"—her voice rose—"we must be as generous in victory as we have been faithful and brave in battle. We must forgive those who lost courage and fell by the wayside.

"Now is a time to heal our wounds, to band together again with every man, woman and child in Arnot. Band together so that next time we'll all be together the whole way through." She stretched out her arms. "I ask you to forgive. I ask you to pity your neighbor, even though he forgot to pity you. I ask you to love your neighbor."

I will, Rosie thought, I will.

"And now," Mother Jones raised her voice joyfully, "let us sing together.

> *"Bring the good old bugle, boys!*
> *We'll sing another song;*
> *Sing it with a spirit*
> *That will start the world along...."*

As the crowd picked up the chant, Mother Jones walked down the steps into the crowd. The cannon roared again. The sky ignited and exploded.

> *"My country, 'tis of thee,*
> *Sweet land of liberty..."*

the trumpets blared.

> *"Of thee I sing...."*

Two miners lifted Mother Jones up on their shoulders.

"Land where my fathers died,
Land of the Pilgrims' pride . . ."

Rosie looked for her family amid the flurry of flags and faces, but she couldn't see them.

"From e-ev-'ry-y mountainside
Le-et freedom ring."

The victory parade whirled down the street in a frenzy of dancing and singing and shouting. Rosie made her way through the crowd, back down the main street to her cousin Mary.

Author's Note

The strike ended on February 23, 1900. By mid-March many evicted families had returned to Arnot, and work began.

The events of this story are true and were reconstructed from articles in the *Blossburg Advertiser*, a local paper that covered the strike in great detail, and from Mother Jones's autobiography. Where the two versions differed, I relied on the newspaper.

Until she was ninety, Mary Harris Jones (1830–1930) devoted her life to helping coal miners in Pennsylvania, Ohio, Alabama, Michigan, Arizona, West Virginia and Colorado. Their plight was drastic. Their low wages were often arbitrarily cut by mine owners. Miners usually lived in company-owned houses, paying excessive rents, and shopped at company-owned stores that charged excessive prices. In most mining towns no other housing or shopping was available. Falls of coal and rock from tunnel roofs, and gas-and-dust explosions, made life underground so dangerous that miners' families never knew if their men would return home from a day's work. Those who survived underground breathed coal dust for twenty and thirty years, and often contracted black lung, a disease that caused difficulty in breathing and often led to death.

As an organizer for the United Mine Workers of America, Mother Jones answered pleas for help from American miners, ignoring danger and hardship. She logged thousands of miles in dusty, uncomfortable trains, sleeping in baggage or cattle cars, to reach coal camps. She ate what the miners ate and slept in their unheated houses and tents. Her enemies called her "the most dangerous woman in America," for her speeches encouraged thousands, and her women's armies, children's marches and parades attracted widespread newspaper coverage and sympathy. Shot at, run out of town and jailed, she always returned to help her beloved miners, who dubbed her "The Miners' Angel."

The songs sung at the parades were favorites of Mother Jones. "Old Hundredth," from the Book of Psalms, retained the same melody, but the words changed over time. "Bring the good old bugle, boys!" comes from the song "Marching Through Georgia." Written in 1865 to celebrate General Sherman's march through the South, it remained popular in the North through the early 1930s. "My Country, 'Tis of Thee," based on the British national anthem, "God Save the King," was published in 1831 and is still sung today.

Bibliography

Atkinson, Linda. *Mother Jones: The Most Dangerous Woman in America*. New York: Crown, 1978.

Blossburg Advertiser. Blossburg, PA: December 1898 to February 1900.

Featherling, Dale. *Mother Jones, The Miners' Angel: A Portrait*. Carbondale, IL: Southern Illinois University Press, 1974.

Foner, Philip S. *Mother Jones Speaks: Collected Writings and Speeches*. New York: Monad Press, 1983.

Jones, Mary Harris. *The Autobiography of Mother Jones*. Chicago: Charles H. Kerr Publishing Co., 1980.

Long, Priscilla. *Mother Jones, Woman Organizer.* Red Sun Press, Cambridge, Mass.: 1976.

Nies, Judith. *Seven Women: Portraits from the American Radical Tradition.* New York: Viking, 1977.

About the Author

DOREEN RAPPAPORT was born in New York City and has taught music and reading in junior high schools in New York and New Rochelle, New York. Ms. Rappaport has created award-winning educational programs and has written two other children's books.

About the Illustrator

JOAN SANDIN has illustrated numerous books for children, including Alan Arkin's *The Lemming Condition* and Clyde Robert Bulla's *Daniel's Duck*. She is also the author-illustrator of *The Long Way to a New Land*. Ms. Sandin was raised in Tucson, Arizona, and now lives in Stockholm, Sweden, with her two children.

Skylark is Riding High with Books for Girls Who Love Horses!

☐ **A HORSE OF HER OWN**
by Joanna Campbell   15564-4 $2.75

Like many 13-year-olds, Penny Rodgers has always longed to ride a horse. Since her parents won't pay for lessons, Penny decides to try her hand at training an old horse named Bones. When she turns him into a champion jumper, Penny proves to everyone that she's serious about riding!

☐ **HORSE CRAZY: THE SADDLE CLUB: BOOK #1   by Bonnie Bryant**   15594-6 $2.75

Beginning with HORSE CRAZY: BOOK #1, this 10-book miniseries tells the stories of three very different girls with one thing in common: horses! Fun-loving Stevie and serious Carole are at Pine Hollow stables for their usual lesson, when they meet another 12-year-old named Lisa. Her elaborate riding outfit prompts the girls to play a practical joke on her. After Lisa retaliates a truce is formed, and so is THE SADDLE CLUB!

- -

Great FREE offer
just for you!

Join SNEAK PEEKS™!

Do you want to know what's new before anyone else? Do you like to read great books about girls just like you? If you do, then you won't want to miss SNEAK PEEKS™! Be the first of your friends to know what's hot ... When you join SNEAK PEEKS™, we'll send you FREE inside information in the mail about the latest books ... *before they're published!* Plus updates on your favorite series, authors, and exciting new stories filled with friendship and fun ... adventure and mystery ... girlfriends and boyfriends.

It's easy to be a member of SNEAK PEEKS™. Just fill out the coupon below ... and get ready for fun! It's FREE! Don't delay—sign up today!

Shop at home
for quality childrens books
and save money, too.

Now you can order books for the whole family from Bantam's latest catalog of hundreds of titles, including many fine children's books. And this special offer gives you the opportunity to purchase a Bantam book for only 50¢. Here's how:

By ordering any five books at the regular price per order, you can also choose any other single book listed (up to a $5.95 value) for just 50¢. Some restrictions do apply, so for further details send for Bantam's listing of titles today!